STOP

TALKING :

DO IT

Teaching Your Child, and Yourself to DO,
Not Just Talk, Whine, Blame and Complain

Elizabeth Wiley MA JD, Pomo Elder

Order this book online at www.trafford.com
or email orders@trafford.com

Most Trafford titles are also available at major online book retailers.

Trafford PUBLISHING® www.trafford.com
North America & international
toll-free: 844 688 6899 (USA & Canada)
fax: 812 355 4082

Our mission is to efficiently provide the world's finest, most comprehensive book publishing service, enabling every author to experience success. To find out how to publish your book, your way, and have it available worldwide, visit us online at www.trafford.com

ISBN: 978-1-6987-1046-4 (SC)
ISBN: 978-1-6987-1045-7 (E)

Print information available on the last page.

Trafford rev. 11/20/2021

STOP TALKING : DO IT

Teaching Your Child, and Yourself to DO, Not Just Talk, Whine, Blame and Complain

1st Edition

INTRODUCTION:

INTRODUCTION:

Our books are written as on ongoing series for high risk youth, veterans, and first responders as well as their parents and those who are raising them.

One of the reasons for starting this series was we, as special needs teachers, as therapists, as Directors of programs and private schools for high risk youth began to recognize how many of the children and youth were children of veterans, grandchildren of veterans, and also first responders.

We then noticed the numbers of minority children and poverty level financial back grounds were the reality for high risk children and youth. We saw children of Mothers who had been as young as NINE at the birth of their child among the high risk students. Whether rich, or poverty level, we saw children of alcohol, sexual, and drug addictions.

We saw children as young as 18 months labeled with an alphabet of mental health disorders, medicated and put into "special schools" where in fact media found they were often warehoused, abused, and not taught at all. Upon seeing a news story about the schools discovered at some of the licensed sites, in which children and teens often did not have desks, or chairs to sit on, let alone proper educational supplies and equipment for special learning program, we joined with others, and designed programs.

We were naive enough to think our work, offered FREE in most cases, would be welcomed especially as we offer it free and often through research projects, but, it was NOT valued or wanted.

What? we asked?

We went back to college and while earning degrees we had apparently NOT needed while working with children of the very rich in expensive private schools, we did research projects to document our findings. To find ways to overcome the problems. Again, our work was NOT valued or wanted.

One of our associates, who had asked many of us to volunteer in a once a month FREE reading program in the local public schools, was held back for almost two years doing paperwork and proving her volunteers, most of them parents of successful children, teens and adults, could read a first five years book and teach parents how to read those books to their own children. She was a Deputy United States Prosecutor, and had recruited friends from all levels of law enforcement, child and family services, education and volunteer groups that served children and families.

None the less, we continued our work, met a fabulous and expensive Psychiatrist who was building his own server system and the first online education project after creating a massive and encompassing medical examination study guide for graduate medical students to assist them in passing global and national medical examinations for licensing.

We worked with a team of citizens and specialists in education who had created a 39 manual project for students, parents and teachers to be able to learn on their own.

This series of books includes ideas, history and thoughts from the students, the parents, and professionals who work with these situations.

Jesus was told, don't have children wasting your time, and he responded, let the children come.

Our work is to bring children to us, and to those who have the heart and love to develop the uniqueness and individuality of each of God's creations. Many of them are of different religions, and beliefs, and many are atheists but believe fully in the wonder and uniqueness of every human.

To all who have helped and continue to help children and anyone wanting to learn, we thank God and we thank you.

Introduction to doing: not just talking

I believe that each of us can be, as Abraham Lincoln, Eleanor Roosevelt as well as others across the centuries and nations have told us, HAPPY. Fulfilled, no matter what. Jesus told us to GO and sin no more. I do not believe he ever meant a list of things to memorize and use to gossip and put other persons down about. I do not believe he meant a long list of things to beat ourselves up to conclude that God made a huge mistake in creating US.

I believe he meant that each of us needs to see SPIRIT in ourselves, and in all others, and make this world the great gift God gave us

One day at a Bible Study talk, I heard a young teen being disrespectful to his Father, and not wanting to be there. After the class I said, "Please come here", little old lady thatI am, he was respectful enough to come over and talk to me I said, "I want to tell you a little story". I told him about my sons, who also did not see any reason, especially the older they got, to study about God, no matter what the religion.

One day my older son, then sixteen, was sent home by the school nurse who wanted a doctor to look at him, he seemed ill to her.

He drove himself to his pediatrician, and came back to say, "it must be bad Mom, he said meet him at the hospital". So we went to the hospital.

The doctor had already had the lab work he had taken at the office analyzed.

My son had a rare, and deadly form of bone and blood cancer. Only two doctors in the whole world were even studying this form of cancer. I told my sons, this is where all the Sunday school and Catholic school, and Hebrew school their Godfather had insisted upon, being Jewish, and all their Native American and Episcopalian, and Assembly of God learning from relatives and going to services with family and friends had to kick in. The doctors told us how grim the statistics were, and that only two doctors in the whole world were even doing research to attempt to understand and treat this type of bone and blood cancer.

One of them had just come, a couple of weeks before, to the cancer research hospital at City of Hope, which thank God was nearby.

Today my son is 52 years old, and been cancer free for decades.

I said to the young man at Bible Study......that day I told my sons that their religious education of many types, had better help us all.

THIS was not the time to decide to find out if there might be a God, or study how people over centuries have found miracles, and given service and enjoyed life, NO MATTER WHAT.

I said, THIS is the time to be grateful you have parents who want you to have a clue when the time for needing a clue comes into life. Most other people hit the hard places and have no clue about having a strength, a friend and Creator bigger than we, who can help us. And how to make that mean something to us.

Over the intervening six years, I have watched that reluctant teen honor his parents and stay in his religious learning programs, finish high school, and go on to college and technical business school. The last I heard, he has his own business. He chose a business that is important, one that people can NOT do for themselves, and in a rural area is needed often by people who live on farms, have large dogs and kennels and other needs for welding and soldering.

This young man found people who had no money to pay, and asked them only to pass around his cards and if asked, give him a good recommendation. He did small jobs, then larger jobs, and asked local contractors to hire him when over burdened by too much work. His resume, and the pictures he took of ALL of his work grew. One day this young man will have the references, experience and skills to get a job with one of those big construction companies, or even get his own license and someday own his own corporation by honoring his parents, learning about something his parents felt would benefit him one day, and helping others to become known. He still helps little old ladies, and others who need his help, he just asks that they make a donation so he has supplies and gas to get to jobs to help others who NEED help, but have no money, and referrals to people who CAN afford to pay for his work.

Chapter One

STOP TALKING, DO IT

Getting Started

If there is one gift we can find for ourselves, and pass along to our children, family and friends, it is to DO what will make us happy. NOW.

AND to stop doing those things that will NOT make us happy.

SORRY, this does not mean, if you don't like something, don't do it.

It does not mean because you "think" it is what you want, do it, without research, and responsibility.

It means to use critical thought, and teach your children to use critical thought to figure out the world in order to BE happy.

It means to accept family in the world, with the environment, with nature, with ALL humans. Many religions and cultures have this ideal, many combine it with service, to our Creator, to each other, to ourselves and FOR ourselves.

COMPLAINING: JUDGING: ADVISING ARROGANTLY

These are all bad habits of "talking" rather than "doing".

Asking for advice you have no intention of considering. Sadly, many people spend time, instead of setting goals, and DOING, wasting other person's lives by asking everyone that will listen what THEY would do. And not doing any of it.

Instead, find a great set of goals, make plans, and DO something.

What DO you want to do? Where DO you want to go? Write some thoughts below:

Consider: If you get into your vehicle and the GPS asks where you want to go, you do NOT get out and ask the first 1200 people to pass by on the street what their advice is before setting a goal for the GPS system. YET, many people do just that in their lives.

Chapter Two

GOALS

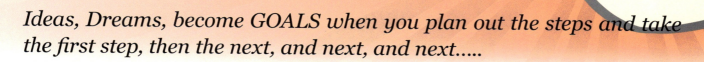

Ideas, Dreams, become GOALS when you plan out the steps and take the first step, then the next, and next, and next.....

Ideas are not GOALS.

Dreams are not GOALS.

A Goal is a place.

All of us talk about dreams, and ideas.......to start the process of DOING IT, list some dreams, ideas, even barest of thoughts below: Look at the chapter before this and see what you wrote down YOU want to do, where YOU want to go. It is suggested that you write, as fast as you can think things up, the one hundred first thoughts of things you want in life......make them clear and short at this point.

WRITE as fast as you can, it is suggested you write them all in one fast ten minute sitting. It is going to be hard... Put down things you might *think are small, not worthy. These might be the ones that come along and can be crossed off your list to help you keep going on the ones that take time and patience, work, and building skill and experience to accomplish.*

IF you do not have time to simply write down what you want, how do you seriously think you are going to accomplish the goals.

100 things I want to accomplish or have in my life.

1

2

3

4

5

6

7

8

9

10

11

12

13

14

15

16

17

18

19

20

21

22

23

24

25

26

27

28

29

30

31

32

33

34

35

36

37

38

39

40

41

42

43

44

45

46

47

48

49

50

51

52

53

54

55

56

57

58

59

60

61

62

63

64

65

66

67

68

69

70

71

72

73

74

75

76

77

78

79

80

81

82

83

Now that you have made your list, read it at least once a week, cross off things you have accomplished, or have been given to you. AND start a notebook listing each of your goals, with space to decide what has to happen for that goal to be accomplished.

For instance, you might have written I want a big chocolate birthday cake, but your birthday is not for many months. You can wait OR you can say, BUT my Grandmother's birthday is tomorrow, and ask other family members to put in some money. You go buy the chocolate cake YOU like at the bakery, with beautiful flowers in a color your Grandmother will love made of frosting on the top of the cake. Cross that chocolate birthday cake off your list!

YOU have learned to get what you want, defined it to just the flavors you want, and gotten others to help you pay for it, maybe they even donated more than was needed, and you can buy drinks your Grandmother will enjoy with the family. AND you can cross big chocolate cake off your goal list.

As you go along, define every line of your goal list.

By the end of your list, some of the items may be strange, or just every day. One of the last items on my list was a certain kind of sandwich. The next day I went to help a friend with a project. When we arrived, she said, OH I had a coupon in the mail, so I went to buy us a sandwich, and they had a special buy one, get one free, and I had a coupon for another.

SO, we ALL had different sandwiches to either cut in three, and share, OR choose from.....one of them was the exact sandwich I had put on my list. Without asking, without paying, and I thanked God for a gift and crossed off another item from my list.

The good thing is, that as you keep working your list, you will define and thank and give gratitude and more of your items will be crossed off the list: accomplished.

Chapter Three

Stop talking about things, DO THEM

The difference between want and need.

BEFORE you begin to sort out dreams and ideas from goals, take a careful look at what is want, and what is NEED.

PEOPLE NEED ten things, says the United Nations Constitution.

A PLACE TO BELONG: NO ONE has the right to make another person without a country, without a place to belong.

AIR, clean air. Every person has a RIGHT to breathe clean, fresh air, every animal, every living creature, tree, bird, insect, animal, reptile or human has a RIGHT to clean air.

WATER, clean, healthy water. A RIGHT to clean and enough water for crops, pets, and farm animals. Wild animals, lakes, creeks, streams, rivers, ponds, and the ocean ALL deserve good unpolluted water.

FOOD. Every creation deserves equal and adequate food for health.

SHELTER: Every creation deserves safe and healthy shelter. Equal shelter. Animals who live in water deserve clean, and healthy water to provide them with both water, air and food to survive and thrive. Animals, and humans that live on dirt, or in forests, or on plains deserve safe and healthy shelter at all times.

JUSTICE: Every Creature and Nature itself deserves to have fair representation in all justice systems. Justice was provided in the US Constitution to give fair and equal justice, to NOT repeat the corrupt and unjust courts of the lands people came from often to stay alive. The people in ALL lands deserve JUSTICE to protect them from people who come to their lands. Included in Justice is the right to FREEDOM as long as not harming others, and to RELIGIOUS FREEDOM as long as NOT forcing the belief of one person or group on to others.

EDUCATION:Every person deserves the RIGHT to an adequate and FREE education to prepare them to live as part of the population of the earth. I believe everyone also deserves the right to learn in a way to help everyone love learning.

MEDICAL CARE:EVERY HUMAN and all animals deserve free and adequate medical care. A freedom to be respected for traditional medical care for each person.

JOBS WITH EQUAL AND ADEQUATE TRAINING FOR CAREERS. Whether a country or area lives in agricultural ways, or ancient ways using their animals to help them survive and taking care of those animals with respect because they are the way of living, or have jobs or careers in modern cities, every person has a right to live and be educated or trained to live, and have choice, not just be enslaved by those who appear to want "it all" at the cost of "all them".

Rights ALL have responsibilities that accompany them. These were included in a series taught around the world by UNICEF volunteer teachers, no one knows how, let alone why the classes, free to every school, were discontinued. IF each human expects to be given and keep these rights, each human must stand up for and support these rights for everyone as well.

This is part of being a light. If we close down, and put a shade on our "light", only to shine on ourselves, in time we are going to find ourselves needing, and no one is going to be there.

There is a famous poem, anonymously written, alleged to have been written by someone who disappeared into the Concentration Camp systems of the Nazi and others. It says something about when "they took away" the others, I did not stand up for them, I was not one of those, and finally when they came for me, there was no one left to stand up for me, they had all been taken.

The Bible itself is filled with centuries of human history in which those who wanted lands or assets simply gave themselves permission, claiming "God on our side" (Bob Dylan song). If we, as individual humans want the rights of every human, we NEED to address the RESPONSIBILITY to not just allow, but to help every other human shine. Sometimes this means standing up and saying "this is not OK".

Martin Luther King, Jr and many others of all different races, genders and cultures have stood up and said, "this is not OK" and changed life for millions. We all NEED to learn about these people, and to have gratitude for them. When we stand up, we want others to stand up with us, and to protect our right to stand up, as well as to stand up for others. This is part of growing into a great adult, even children and teens have been honored for these acts of standing up for others.

Chapter Four

WANTS

Breaking down some of our wants, and finding out if we truly want them.

Wants ALL have responsibilities that accompany them.

Teach yourself, and your children to find out BEFORE getting something you WANT if you really need it. The responsibilities might be much more than you want to take on.

For instance: If your child wants a puppy, pony or other living being:

For those NOT already familiar with our programs, children and adults utilize contracts, and negotiations rather than screaming, insulting and heartbreaking arguments to reach resolution of problems between children and adults. The skills and background of contracts are discussed at length in others of our inclusion books.

Create a contract with your child about WHEN and WHAT has to happen BEFORE considering that reality.

In the book we use to teach people about living beings, including children, "A HORSE IS NOT A BICYCLE" the lessons of this area are deeply discussed. IS YOUR CHILD mature enough to understand that living beings are not stuffed toys? Or trendy toys seen on television or a movie? You may ask the child's teacher, Grandparents, Aunts, Uncles, Neighbors for advice on this evaluation point.

IS the child able to readily accept that whats mine is mine, and what's someone else's property is to be respected, cared for, and NOT coveted. This means that YOUR child will not be bringing a living being into a dangerous situation due to young, or mal-adapted siblings or adults in the home. On the other hand, it is necessary for every adult to learn that it is NOT the responsibility of any child, or teen to do without because a sibling is disabled or ill......Children and teens can be helped to develop love and empathy to GIVE to siblings and others, but will not grow and flower if they do without due to a sibling, or parent with health, addiction or other issues.

Children NEED to understand that what they WANT is not always a good choice for other living beings.

Children who DO NOT learn this are the ones who are most likely one day, to dump an unwanted baby, or toddler on your front porch, or couch and go off to have "more fun".

DO YOU LIVE in an environment safe and healthy for the wanted animal??? Children can, and need to, understand that even when you own your own home, in America at least, laws and rules are created together and need to be adhered to, whether it interferes with what your CHILD wants or not.

If for instance you live in a NO PETS apartment complex, and YOUR FAMILY will be evicted if you have pets, the answer to "can I have a puppy" is NO. YOU would not be happy if your landlord said, "OK, kids love pets" and let everyone have pets, and then sent everyone a raise in rent of one hundred dollars a month per household to pay the increased insurance demanded by the city and insurance company for buildings that allow pets.

NOR would you be happy if everyone had pets, and someone had a teenager who brought in palsies during the day while parents were at work, and one of them brought in a horribly abused, fighting dog and it tore YOUR child into shreds. Especially if you found out there was NO insurance except your own renters insurance, which if used for any reason automatically goes up in price.

When your child learns pets mean responsibility, NOT how can I sneak around the rules, your child will be well on the way to NOT being a drunk driver, or criminal, or having unwanted kids to dump on you, or get taken away by the Court and adopted out.

This type of responsible investigation of ANY wish or want is important as a lifetime skill.

YOU do not do the investigation. If your child is old enough for a pet, that child is old enough to use a smart phone or computer to find answers.

IF you think it is cute to see a child dragging a little dog around by its neck, YOU are not mature enough to own a pet, and YOU are the one who will be arrested should someone call animal control on you, or the police see this abuse, and YOU are taken to court. Should an animal support rescue go to court to take the animal away from your abusive child, it is YOU that is legally responsible, it is YOU that can be fined, or put in jail.

Is your child old enough to watch You Tube, or other media video and LEARN HOW TO PROPERLY train a puppy or other pet??? Is your child competent enough to read books or online material to help get answers to pet problems???

IF you decide YOU want a pet, YOU write down the steps and YOU make sure your child helps you with the responsibility of raising that pet. AND you let them know, abuse the pet, and YOU will find a new safe home for the animal. Then YOU make sure that pet is always properly cared for, which does NOT include dumping it off somewhere to be abused, over, starve, or killed by mentally ill animal abusers. Do not think the pound finds them homes, they do their best, then the animal, which has a broken heart is killed because the pound is over filled.

It is up to you to help your child shine a light of humane treatment of animals and others.

THE REASON THIS CHAPTER IS HERE is to help YOU stop talking about what YOU want, and learn to balance if what YOU want is as good for someone, or something else should YOU try to grab what YOU want, rather than reconfigure what it is YOU really want, and need, and redefine the want on that number to be responsible AND still OK for you to have. It is here to remind you that the things you allow your child or teen to do come on YOU, legally and financially, if you do not care about the reality that YOU are allowing your child or teen to grow up selfish and without responsibility for their actions.

YOU can change every relationship you have. Today. Go meet with the person, write them a text, but let them know new rules are in town. The list the changes clearly. Listen to complaints, but be prepared to defend YOU and other people's rights.

Go back to your notebook and re-read every remaining goal. What are you asking that is NOT your right to have, what are you asking that IS your right to have, what has to happen to balance rights and responsibilities to make the goal achievable yet not just selfish.

Chapter Five

FIND a way

Go back over each goal left in your notebook each day, or once a week, as YOU decide.

Begin to make a list for each goal, you may need to make a special page for some of the goals, eventually some goals may need their own notebook!

For example: I want a certain kind of dinner, from a certain restaurant, but think it is way too expensive. Discuss this with yourself. IS it just too expensive? Do YOU deserve a treat from yourself, and start to think of ways to earn the money to get that goal removed from the list. Do you want anyone else to come with you? As with my sandwich, you might ask someone if they want to come along, THEY might say, hey, I got a gift certificate for that restaurant, if you pay the tip, I will pay for the two meals. You just never know how your goal is going to met.

Maybe you will send a text to each member of your family, and say "I am working for a certain goal, and need to make some extra money, do you have some chores, or a household job, like painting, or a big spring window wash I can help you with to earn part of the money?"

Either here, or in a page of your notebook, write comments for each of your goals that have not been met.

REMEMBER as you read over your list, to be grateful for each goal met!!! AND for each goal you decided to take off the list because you had no right to that goal in the first place. Be grateful for your own growth that helped you see that marrying your favorite star was a LOT unfair to the existing spouse and children, and possibly even the star........that person might love their family, and not need you coming around trying to butt your way in. Put something else on the list: example: I want a life long relationship with......and maybe take some classes on being mature enough to meet, and love a person who is mature and loving enough to want a lifelong relationship. If all you want is a one night stand, put on a tee shirt or jacket that says so, and go to a sleazy bar.

Chapter Six

Stop complaining about no help

If you are the only one left on Mars, like the movie, decide what you NEED to do, and what NEEDS to be done to get what you want, and start a plan.

Step by Step, anything is a cinch. Dr. Robert Schuller. Hour of Power.

I had an equine therapy program. I never intended to have one, The thought came to me, and I started, it, one horse and me, and kids along the way. At one point I had moved four horses to my friends stable, that had been unused for some years. She had asked me to come, and help her clear out her back acre because the fire department was telling her it was becoming a fire hazard. I had had my horses at stables where they were fed, cleaned, and even turned out if I was out of town.

Now I had to have feed and hay delivered, and clean and feed myself every day, besides building up the shelters and barns again. A hay truck deliver thirty bales of hay, and 15 bags of pellets, along with other supplements once a month. BUT, I had to move all from the top of the driveway down to the barn after they unloaded it. I thought of that old saying"inch by inch" anything's a cinch" as I began to learn how to move all that hay and feed about a block down hill and then up the stairs to the feed room. I also was working full time to pay for the program I gave free to high risk youth.

ANYONE can look at something and figure out how to break it down into doable pieces and one by one get the job done. I have moved bales of hay one flake at a time when I came out of surgery, or back from back injuries from being hit by drunk drivers. I took my older son's garden van, which I could step in to, and had the feed store load two or three days of hay and feed in. I brought grocery bags and put one flake, or a serving of supplements or pellets in bags and carried them down the hill to the paddocks and fed the horses.

Blessed were the days I had equine therapy students and their parents who came and helped. I also had to cut down a lot of trees that had overgrown the area, many had died, to clear the property for a fire department clearance receipt. I learned how to tie parts of trees to each other, or to my truck and chain saw them in pieces, then chain saw the pieces and put them in the firewood pile or trash cans or recycling pile as the stable owner wanted.

YOU can figure out how to break down anything YOU need to do, where to get started, THEN get started. Sooner than you think, the whole truckload is moved safely into the feed barn, or whatever YOUR need to accomplish towards your goal.

In YOUR notebook, list ONE of your items, and draw out what it is going to take to get the goal completed. Break down each part, first on the drawing, then on the notebook page, and figure out how to break down each part and complete them systematically to reach each tiny goal, and eventually the goal.

Break down each of your remaining goals as you go along, you are going to be surprised how the 100 in your original list are being met. Create a daily, weekly and monthly planner to reach the yearly goals.

Some goals, such as going to medical school, or joining an environmental protection project take time, but you can work towards them each day. If a plane ticket to a place you want to travel to is part of a goal, list the cost in your notebook, break it down into dollars per day over one year. You will be surprised that often just ONE soda, or mineral water or coffee is the price each day for a year to completely pay for your travel ticket.

Chapter Seven

Moving ahead with "miracles"

Be grateful for each step towards goals that occurs. Be grateful for each goal met. TELL people about your "miracles" and how grateful you are.

Sit down, write in one or two sentences below your main goal. In your notebook write one or two sentences for each goal. Say THANK YOU for each goal already crossed off the list.

Example: If someone says, what do you do, think of one of the top ten goals and say......I am learning how to surf. I am getting ready to travel around the world. Each time you say it, go over how close you are getting. Maybe you have given up just ONE soft drink or coffee a day and now have nearly $1000 in a special account for your goal.

Chapter Eight

SEE YOURSELF THERE

Create ways to "see yourself there" fake it until you make it, be grateful for each step closer you get to the goals.

As you create real hard material things to direct your inner GPS towards your goals, you NEED to talk to people. Talk to those who support your dreams. Those who try to tell you why and how you are not going to make it.......do NOT talk to them about your dreams. THEY are dream killers. This does not mean do not be friends with family and friends who are negative, it simply means keep your dreams and goals for people who support you.

Talk to the guys on the train, the tram, the bus, waiting in line at an amusement park or theatre now that they are open. Talk to your waiter or waitress for a moment. You NEVER know who people are, and who they know. One of them just might say "MY friend(mother, father, old room mate, etc" might give you some really good advice. Their person "might" help you figure out how to get where you are going faster and *more successfully. Again, as the Bible says about those who do NOT support your work, or thoughts, or dreams, move on, and wash the dust of them off your feet. Matthew 10;14. cast the dust off your feet and move on. Jesus was talking about people who denied support to his disciples as they came to teach in new towns, but YOU can apply it to those who speak against you, do not take their negativity as a burden to yourself.*

Design and BUY a vehicle magnet with your new business name and logo on it. Buy yourself a tee shirt and maybe create stationary to send out letters or emails to get the legal parts of what you are doing completed. All of these things help YOU feel more positive about your making your dreams come true.

Find out what legal steps you might need to take to get going. Several large online law firms specialize in this type of law for your own state and will direct you to firms that do the same for federal law if it applies.

Make a list of some things YOU can do to make yourself feel positive and moving towards your goals.

Chapter Nine

Take each step

Remember that every journey begins with that first step. You can NOT get into your vehicle and say "I dunno" when the GPS asks you where you want to get to. YOU can not get to where YOU want to go unless you make it clear where and what it is you want, or need.

Your vehicle is NOT going to jump over the freeway overpass and take its own route once you set the GPS, YOU have to remind yourself not to jump over the overpass no matter how things get hard, or what obstacles get in your way.

Be Prepared: For each goal, in your notebook, list obstacles as they arise, do NOT make up a list of what "might" happen, acorns 'might" fall on your head, but it is unlikely. As those obstacles arise, reset your daily, weekly and longer goal plans. Keep going.

GO join a credit union or bank. TALK to the manager and ask how that person and their bank or credit union can help you. If you want a vehicle, or home, or business loan, ASK, do you have first time buyer plans.

Find out about taking loans against your own money when you have built credit with that institution. ASK if the city, county, state or Federal government has any special loans or grants to do what you want to do.

Go to the Small Business Association websites and local offices and ask for advice.

Get a new page for every goal and create a positive GPS list to go out and find help for yourself.

REWARD yourself when you overcome obstacles, List ten ways you can reward yourself that do NOT cost money if you are saying for some of your goals.

List people who will support you by awarding you when you get over an obstacle, or meet an objective......figure out ways to support and award them as they meet their goals as well. The more you are with people who DO instead of complain and blame, the more your dreams will begin to come true.

Chapter Ten

Closing:

In closing never forget to be grateful, and never forget to share the go get it attitude instead of sit and slump in self pity.

When people discourage you, smile and let their dust be brushed off your shoulders and heart.

Find people who DO instead wish, hope, whine, blame complain.

A closing story to share: On my list for this year was to write and publish some workbooks for classes I teach......got a stimulus check, invested it in me!

I. wanted to visit with my two sons, for a three of us picture and hug because its been. eighteen years in our busy lives since we did that. My older son woke me early.....he NEVER wakes me up, and I do not get up early. He said check y our. email. We both gotten a grant. Off to our family reunion...AND went to some business appointments soon the way out and back......good connections. and start back after COVID *restrictions. Gratitude! Two emails, forgot about them and then checks for each of us!!! God bless.*

Closing and Other Books by Author and team

Closing:

All of our group of books, and workbooks contain some work pages, and/ or suggestions for the reader, and those teaching these books to make notes, to go to computer, and libraries and ask others for information to help these projects work their best.

To utilize these to their fullest, make sure YOU model the increased thoughts and availability of more knowledge to anyone you share these books and workbooks with in classes, or community groups.

Magazines are, as noted in most of the books, a wonderful place to look for and find ongoing research and information. Online search engines often bring up new research in the areas, and newly published material.

We all have examples of how we learned and who it was that taught us.

One of the strangest lessons I have learned was walking to a shoot in downtown Los Angeles. The person who kindly told me to park my truck in Pasadena, and take the train had been unaware that the weekend busses did NOT run early in the morning when the crews had to be in to set up. That person, being just a participant, was going much later in the day, taking a taxi, and had no idea how often crews do NOT carry purses with credit cards, large amounts of cash, and have nowhere to carry those items, because the crew works hard, and fast during a set up and tear down and after the shoot are TIRED and not looking to have to find items that have been left around, or stolen.

As I walked, I had to travel through an area of Los Angeles that had become truly run down and many homeless were encamped about and sleeping on the sidewalks and in alleys. I saw a man, that having worked in an ER for many years I realized was DEAD. I used to have thoughts about people who did not notice people needing help, I thought, this poor man, this is probably the most peace he has had in a long time. I prayed for him and went off to my unwanted walk across town. As I walked, I thought about myself, was I just heartless, or was I truly thinking this was the only moment of peace this man had had for a long time and just leaving him to it. What good were upset neighbors, and police, fire trucks and ambulances going to do. He was calmly, eyes open, staring out at a world that had failed him while alive, why rush to disturb him now that nothing could be done.

I did make sure he was DEAD. He was, quite cold rigid.

I learned that day that it is best to do what a person needs, NOT what we need.

Learning is about introspection and grounding of material. Passing little tests on short term memory skills and not knowing what it all means is NOT education, or teaching.

As a high school student, in accelerated Math and Science programs, in which I received 4.0 grades consistently, I walked across a field, diagonally, and suddenly all that math and science made sense, it was not just exercises on paper I could throw answers back on paper, but I realized had NO clue as to what it all really meant.

OTHER BOOKS by this author, and team

Most, if not all, of these books are written at a fourth grade level. FIrst, the author is severely brain damaged from a high fever disease caused by a sample that came in the mail, without a warning that it had killed during test marketing. During the law suit, it was discovered that the corporation had known prior to mailing out ten million samples, WITHOUT warnings of disease and known deaths, and then NOT telling anyone after a large number of deaths around the world started. Second, the target audience is high risk youth, and young veterans, most with a poor education before signing into, or being drafted into the military as a hope Many of our veterans are Vietnam or WWII era.

Maybe those recruiting promises would come true. They would be trained, educated, and given chance for a home, and to protect our country and its principles. Watch the movies Platoon, and Born on the Fourth of July as well as the Oliver Stone series on history to find out how these dreams were meet.

DO NOT bother to write and tell us of grammar or spelling errors. We often wrote these books and workbooks fast for copyrights. We had learned our lessons about giving our material away when one huge charity asked us for our material, promising a grant, Instead, we heard a couple of years later they had built their own VERY similar project, except theirs charged for services, ours were FREE, and theirs was just for a small group, ours was training veterans and others to spread the programs as fast as they could.. They got a Nobel Peace prize. We keep saying we are not bitter, we keep saying we did not do our work to get awards, or thousands of dollars of grants....but, it hurts. Especially when lied to and that group STILL sends people to US for help when they can not meet the needs, or the veterans and family can not afford their "charitable" services. One other group had the nerve to send us a Cease and Desist using our own name. We said go ahead and sue, we have proof of legal use of this name for decades. That man had the conscience to apologize, his program was not even FOR veterans or first responders, or their families, nor high risk kids. But we learned. Sometimes life is very unfair.

We got sued again later for the same issue. We settled out of Court as our programs were just restarting and one of the veterans said, let's just change that part of the name and keep on training veterans to run their own programs. Smart young man.

Book List:

DRAGON KITES and other stories:

The Grandparents Story list will add 12 new titles this year. We encourage every family to write their own historic stories. That strange old Aunt who when you listen to her stories left a rich and well regulated life in the Eastern New York coastal fashionable families to learn Telegraph messaging and go out to the old west to LIVE her life. That old Grandfather or Grandmother who was sent by family in other countries torn by war to pick up those "dollars in the streets" as noted in the book of that title.

Books in publication, or out by summer 2021

Carousel Horse: A Children's book about equine therapy and what schools MIGHT be and are in special private programs.

Carousel Horse: A smaller version of the original Carousel Horse, both contain the workbooks and the screenplays used for on site stable programs as well as lock down programs where the children and teens are not able to go out to the stables.

Spirit Horse II: This is the work book for training veterans and others interested in starting their own Equine Therapy based programs. To be used as primary education sites, or for supplementing public or private school programs. One major goal of this book is to copyright our founding material, as we gave it away freely to those who said they wanted to help us get grants. They did not. Instead they built their own programs, with grant money, and with donations in small, beautiful stables and won....a Nobel Peace Prize for programs we invented. We learned our lessons, although we do not do our work for awards, or grants, we DO not like to be ripped off, so now we copyright.

Reassessing and Restructuring Public Agencies; This book is an over view of our government systems and how they were expected to be utilized for public betterment. This is a Fourth Grade level condemnation of a PhD dissertation that was not accepted be because the mentor thought it was "against government" .. The first paragraph noted that a request had been made, and referrals given by the then White House.

Reassessing and Restructuring Public Agencies; TWO. This book is a suggestive and creative work to give THE PEOPLE the idea of taking back their government and making the money spent and the agencies running SERVE the PEOPLE ;not politicians. This is NOT against government, it is about the DUTY of the PEOPLE to oversee and control government before it overcomes us.

Could This Be Magic? A Very Short Book. This is a very short book of pictures and the author's personal experiences as the Hall of Fame band VAN HALEN practiced in her garage. The pictures are taken by the author, and her then five year old son. People wanted copies of the pictures, and permission was given to publish them to raise money for treatment and long term Veteran homes.

Carousel TWO: Equine therapy for Veterans. publication pending 2021

Carousel THREE: Still Spinning: Special Equine therapy for women veterans and single mothers. This book includes TWELVE STEPS BACK FROM BETRAYAL for soldiers who have been sexually assaulted in the active duty military and help from each other to heal, no matter how horrible the situation. publication pending 2021

LEGAL ETHICS: AN OXYMORON. A book to give to lawyers and judges you feel have not gotten the justice of American Constitution based law (Politicians are great persons to gift with this book). Publication late 2021

PARENTS CAN LIVE and raise great kids.

Included in this book are excerpts from our workbooks from KIDS ANONYMOUS and KIDS JR, and A PARENTS PLAIN RAP (to teach sexuality and relationships to their children. This program came from a copyrighted project thirty years ago, which has been networked into our other programs. This is our training work book. We asked AA what we had to do to become a real Twelve Step program as this is considered a quasi twelve step program children and teens can use to heal BEFORE becoming involved in drugs, sexual addiction, sexual trafficking and relationship woes, as well as unwanted, neglected and abused or having children murdered by parents not able to deal with the reality of parenting. Many of our original students were children of abuse and neglect, no matter how wealthy. Often the neglect was by society itself when children lost parents to illness, accidents or addiction. We were told, send us a copy and make sure you call it quasi. The Teens in the first programs when surveyed for the outcome research reports said, WE NEEDED THIS EARLIER. SO they helped younger children invent KIDS JR. Will be republished in 2021 as a documentary of the work and success of these projects.

Addicted To Dick. This is a quasi Twelve Step program for women in domestic violence programs mandated by Courts due to repeated incidents and danger, or actual injury or death of their children.

Addicted to Dick 2018 This book is a specially requested workbook for women in custody, or out on probation for abuse to their children, either by themselves or their sexual partners or spouses. The estimated national number for children at risk at the time of request was three million across the nation. During Covid it is estimated that number has risen. Homelessness and undocumented families that are unlikely to be reported or found are creating discussion of a much larger number of children maimed or killed in these domestic violence crimes. THE most important point in this book is to force every local school district to train teachers, and all staff to recognize children at risk, and to report their family for HELP, not punishment. The second most important part is to teach every child on American soil to know to ask for help, no matter that parents, or other relatives or known adults, or unknown adults have threatened to kill them for "telling". Most, if not all paramedics, emergency rooms, and police and fire stations are trained to protect the children and teens, and get help for the family.. PUNISHMENT is not the goal, eliminating childhood abuse and injury or death at the hands of family is the goal of all these projects. In some areas JUDGES of child and family courts were taking training and teaching programs themselves to HELP. FREE..

Addicted to Locker Room BS. This book is about MEN who are addicted to the lies told in locker rooms and bars. During volunteer work at just one of several huge juvenile lock downs, where juveniles who have been convicted as adults, but are waiting for their 18th birthday to be sent to adult prisons, we noticed that the young boys and teens had "big" ideas of themselves, learned in locker rooms and back alleys. Hundreds of these young boys would march, monotonously around the enclosures, their lives over. often facing long term adult prison sentences.

The girls, we noticed that the girls, for the most part were smart, had done well in school, then "something" happened. During the years involved in this volunteer work I saw only ONE young girl who was so mentally ill I felt she was not reachable, and should be in a locked down mental health facility for help; if at all possible, and if teachers, and others had been properly trained, helped BEFORE she gotten to that place, lost in the horror and broken of her childhood and early teen years.

We noticed that many of the young women in non military sexual assault healing programs were "betrayed" in many ways, by step fathers, boyfriends, even fathers, and mothers by either molestation by family members, or allowing family members or friends of parents to molest these young women, often as small children. We asked military sexually assaulted young women to begin to volunteer to help in the programs to heal the young girls and teens, it helped heal them all.

There was NOTHING for the boys that even began to reach them until our research began on the locker room BS theory of life destruction and possible salvaging by the boys themselves, and men in prisons who helped put together something they thought they MIGHT have heard before they ended up in prison.

Americans CAN Live Happily Ever After. Parents edition.One

Americans CAN Live Happily Ever After. Children's edition Two.

Americans CAN Live Happily Ever After. Three. After Covid. This book includes "Welcome to America" a requested consult workbook for children and youth finding themselves in cages, auditoriums on cots, or in foster group homes or foster care of relatives or non-relatives with NO guidelines for their particular issues. WE ASKED the kids, and they helped us write this fourth grade level workbook portion of this book to help one another and each other. Written in a hurry! We were asked to use our expertise in other youth programs, and our years of experience teaching and working in high risk youth programs to find something to help.

REZ CHEESE Written by a Native American /WASP mix woman. Using food, and thoughts on not getting THE DIABETES, stories are included of a childhood between two worlds.

REZ CHEESE TWO A continuation of the stress on THE DIABETES needing treatment and health care from birth as well as recipes, and stories from Native America, including thoughts on asking youth to help stop the overwhelming numbers of suicide by our people.

BIG LIZ: LEADER OF THE GANG Stories of unique Racial Tension and Gang Abatement projects created when gangs and racial problems began to make schools unsafe for our children.

DOLLARS IN THE STREETS, ghost edited for author Lydia Caceras, the first woman horse trainer at Belmont Park.

95 YEARS of TEACHING:

A book on teaching, as opposed to kid flipping

Two teachers who have created and implemented systems for private and public education a combined 95 plus years of teaching talk about experiences and realities and how parents can get involved in education for their children. Included are excerpts from our KIDS ANONYMOUS and KIDS JR workbooks of over 30 years of free youth programs.

A HORSE IS NOT A BICYCLE. A book about pet ownership and how to prepare your children for responsible pet ownership and along the way to be responsible parents. NO ONE needs to own a pet, or have a child, but if they make that choice, the animal, or child deserves a solid, caring forever home.

OLD MAN THINGS and MARE'S TALES. this is a fun book about old horse trainers I met along the way. My husband used to call the old man stories "old man things", which are those enchanting and often very effective methods of horse, pet, and even child rearing. I always said I brought up my children and my students the same as I had trained horses and dogs......I meant that horses and dogs had taught me a lot of sensible, humane ways to bring up an individual, caring, and dream realizing adult who was HAPPY and loved.

STOP TALKING, DO IT

ALL of us have dreams, intentions, make promises. This book is a workbook from one of our programs to help a person make their dreams come true, to build their intentions into goals, and realities, and to keep their promises. One story from this book, that inspired the concept is a high school kid, now in his sixties, that was in a special ed program for drug abuse and not doing well in school. When asked, he said his problem was that his parents would not allow him to buy a motorcycle. He admitted that he did not have money to buy one, insure one, take proper driver's education and licensing examinations to own one, even though he had a job. He was asked to figure out how much money he was spending on drugs. Wasting his own money, stealing from his parents and other relatives, and then to figure out, if he saved his own money, did some side jobs for neighbors and family until he was 18, he COULD afford the motorcycle and all it required to legally own one. In fact, he did all, but decided to spend the money on college instead of the motorcycle when he graduated from high school. His priorities had changed as he learned about responsible motorcycle ownership and risk doing the assignments needed for his special ed program. He also gave up drugs, since his stated reason was he could not have a motorcycle, and that was no longer true, he COULD have a motorcycle, just had to buy it himself, not just expect his parents to give it to him.

Printed in the United States
by Baker & Taylor Publisher Services